PIXIE TRICKS

Sporty
Sprite

· by ·
TRACEY
WEST

A
LITTLE APPLE
PAPERBACK

SCHOLASTIC INC.
New York Toronto London Auckland Sydney
Mexico City New Delhi Hong Kong

For Jessica, a friend to fairies —
and someone who could definitely
teach Sport a lesson.
— T.W.

Book design by Dawn Adelman

ISBN 0-439-17982-3

Cover illustration by James Bernardin
Interior and sticker illustrations by Thea Kliros

12 11 10 9 8   5/0

Printed in the U.S.A.   40
First Scholastic printing, January 2001

·: CONTENTS :·

Sprite is a Pixie Tricker,

Sent by the fairy queen.

He's after fourteen pixies.

They're troublesome and mean!

Sprite asked for help from Violet,

A clever little girl.

She'll help him trick the pixies,

And send them to their world.

They've tricked seven pixies up 'til now,

With seven more to go.

Will Sprite and Violet trick them all?

Keep reading and you'll know!

Chapter One
Seven More to Go

"Seven more pixies to go," Violet Briggs sang as she walked home from school. "Seven more pixies to go."

Violet made up the tune as she went along. She felt a little silly, but she couldn't help herself. It seemed all she could think about lately were pixies and fairies.

It all started when she met Sprite, a fairy from the Otherworld. Sprite had asked Violet to help him trick fourteen fairies. The

fairies had escaped from his world. They were causing lots of trouble.

Violet had agreed to help Sprite. They had tricked seven pixies so far and sent them back home.

"Seven more pixies to go," Violet sang again.

Tricking pixies was not easy. Each fairy had to be tricked in a different way. Violet never knew what would happen next. But today would be different. Today she knew exactly what would happen.

First she'd do her math homework. Then she and Sprite would work on their plan to catch Hinky Pink. Hinky Pink was a fairy who could control the weather. She and Sprite had been trying to catch him from the start.

Then Violet's dad would make spaghetti. He did that every Monday.

It sounded like a good plan. A normal afternoon — with no surprises.

Violet skipped to the back of her yellow house. She walked up the steps to the second floor.

Violet's dad gave her a hug.

"Mom's working tonight," he said. "How about I make some spaghetti?"

Violet smiled. "Great!" she said. "I'll be in my room."

Violet skipped down the hallway. She opened the door to her room.

A tiny fairy sat on her dresser.

"Who are you?" the fairy asked.

Chapter Two
Ragamuffin

Violet froze. Then she quickly closed the door behind her.

The fairy had two red braids. She wore a colorful dress made of different patches stitched together. She wore one red sock and one blue sock.

"Who are *you*?" Violet asked her.

Sprite flew up to Violet. He looked excited. Sprite had shimmery wings and pale

green skin. His clothes looked like they were made of brown leaves.

"This is Ragamuffin," Sprite said. "She is a pixie. She likes to steal socks. You know how sometimes you can't find socks that match? That's because of Ragamuffin."

Ragamuffin frowned. "I don't steal them. I just borrow them," she said. "Of course, sometimes I forget to bring them back."

Violet thought fast. They had to catch this pixie! But how could they trick her?

"Sprite, what should we —" Violet started to say.

"Ragamuffin and I have been having a nice talk," he said. "She's telling me all about socks." Then Sprite slipped something into Violet's hand.

Ragamuffin smiled. "Socks are super!" she said. "They're soft. And pretty. I like socks with stripes. Or dots. Once I found a sock with little frogs on it. It was so cute. . . ."

"Tell me more!" Sprite said.

Ragamuffin chattered on about socks. Violet secretly looked at what was in her hand. It was the *Book of Tricks*! The book told how to trick all the escaped pixies.

Violet knew what Sprite wanted her to do. If Sprite could keep Ragamuffin busy, Violet could find out how to trick Ragamuffin.

Violet sat down at her desk and turned her back to Ragamuffin. Then Violet looked in the book. She had to act fast. Some pixies were very smart. They were able to figure out how Sprite and Violet were going to trick them. That made the job harder.

Violet remembered when Jolt, the gremlin who liked video games, had figured out the trick. In the end, they got lucky. Her cousin, Leon, tricked Jolt by accident.

Maybe Ragamuffin didn't know about the

trick. It seemed that all she could think about was socks. They might have a chance.

Violet found Ragamuffin's page in the *Book of Tricks*. "Socks are what Ragamuffin loves the best. If she wears clothes that match, you'll pass this test!"

Violet looked at Ragamuffin. Her clothes did not match. Her socks didn't match either. She could use a new outfit. But what?

"I like fuzzy socks, and rainbow socks, and socks with kitties on them, and . . ." Ragamuffin talked and talked.

Then Violet had an idea. She ran to her toy box. She took out a box of clothes for her doll, Traci Teen. The doll and Ragamuffin were about the same size.

Violet looked in the box until she found the perfect outfit. A purple shirt. A white

skirt with purple stripes. A pair of purple
stockings. White boots. A perfect match!

"Socks with hearts are nice. So are socks
with flowers," Ragamuffin was telling Sprite.

"Yes, yes, tell me more," Sprite said.

Violet walked over to the pixie. "Excuse
me," Violet said. "I see you like clothes. I
thought maybe you would like these." She
held out the doll clothes.

Ragamuffin stopped talking. Her eyes got
wide.

"That's a super outfit!" she said. She hopped up and took the clothes from Violet.

"Why don't you try it on?" Violet asked. She crossed her fingers for luck. If Ragamuffin put on the clothes, she would be tricked. Then she would go back to the Otherworld.

"Sure," Ragamuffin said.

Violet and Sprite looked at each other. They were going to trick Ragamuffin! This was the easiest pixie trick yet.

Suddenly, Violet's cousin, Leon, burst into her room.

"Violet! Sprite!" Leon cried. He was out of breath. "Come with me! It's an emergency!"

Chapter Three
Leon's Emergency

"We've got to get to the school field!" Leon said. "Right now!"

Leon was the only other person who knew about Sprite. Violet thought he was always getting in the way. Like now.

"Leon, we're in the middle of something here," Violet said. She looked behind her.

A light shimmered where Ragamuffin once had stood. But Ragamuffin was gone. So were the clothes.

"She's gone!" Sprite cried.

"Who's gone?" Leon asked.

"Ragamuffin," Violet explained. "She's a pixie who steals socks. We were about to trick her."

"If she's gone, then you did trick her," Leon said. "Now you've got to come with me." He grabbed Violet's arm.

Sprite fluttered his wings. "I'm not sure if we tricked her," Sprite said. "I didn't see her disappear."

"Let's check the *Book of Tricks*," Violet said. She picked up the little book. "If she was tricked, her picture will be in here now."

Leon's face turned bright red. "You don't understand! This isn't some sock-stealing pixie. This is worse. Much, much worse. Just come to the field!"

Sprite reached into the bag around his

waist. He took out a handful of shiny dust. Pixie dust.

"All right, Leon!" he said.

Sprite threw the pixie dust over their heads. "To the school field!" he yelled.

Chapter Four
Magic on the Field

Violet closed her eyes and held her nose. The pixie dust tickled. She thought she would never get used to it.

The tingling stopped. Violet opened her eyes. They were outside the school field.

There were three field areas behind the school. There was a soccer field, a baseball diamond, and a grassy field where kids could play whatever they wanted.

Sprite flew into Violet's pocket. He couldn't risk being seen.

"All right, Leon," Violet said. "What's the emergency?"

"Just look!" Leon said. He pointed to a group of kids playing kickball.

A boy kicked the ball. But the ball didn't zoom straight ahead. Instead, it zoomed up! Then it flew over the boy's head and landed behind him.

"I guess that's weird," Violet said. "But it's not really an emergency."

"There's more!" Leon said. He took off toward the baseball field.

A boy threw a ball to a girl at bat. The girl hit the ball.

Poof! The baseball turned into white dust. It covered the girl.

"My goodness!" Sprite said.

Violet watched closely. This was definitely more than weird.

Someone threw a new ball to the pitcher. He threw the ball again.

The girl swung at the ball. But this time, her bat wiggled as if it were made of jelly! She missed the ball.

"See what I mean?" Leon asked. "It's been like this all afternoon. None of the sports equipment will work. They're all messed up. I bet a really bad fairy's doing this."

Violet turned back to the kids who were playing kickball. Some kids nearby were throwing a Frisbee. The Frisbee flew through the sky. Then it stopped in midair! The Frisbee floated for a minute. Then it fell to the ground.

Sprite peeked out of Violet's pocket.

"I think Leon's right," Sprite said. "It looks like one of the escaped pixies is behind this. The sports equipment seems enchanted."

"Who's doing it?" Violet asked. "Is it Ragamuffin?"

Sprite shook his head. "She likes socks. I don't think she cares about sports. It must be someone new."

"We should look in the *Book of Tricks*," Violet said.

Then loud cheers came from the soccer field. A crowd of kids was watching a team practice.

"Let's check it out," Leon said.

Violet ran after Leon. She went to the front of the crowd.

The girls on the team all wore red T-shirts. Violet knew them from school.

The girls were practicing shooting balls into an open goal. But they weren't standing close to the goal at all. They were all the way across the field!

"My turn!" said a girl named Mandy. She wore her blond hair in two ponytails.

Mandy put the black-and-white soccer ball down on the ground.

Violet waited to see what would happen. Would the ball explode? Would it disappear?

Wham! Mandy kicked the ball.

It flew through the air. It soared all the way across the field.

Violet kept waiting for the ball to drop.

It didn't. It kept going. And going.

Then it dropped right into the goal!

The girls on the team high-fived Mandy.

"We are going to win every game!" Mandy said. "We're magic!"

Chapter Five
A Sprite Named Sport

"Mandy doesn't know this," Sprite whispered to Violet, "but they really *are* magic."

"We need to find out more," Violet said.

"Let's go down by the goal," Sprite suggested.

Violet walked away from the crowd, down to the other end of the field. Luckily, no one was nearby. Sprite peeked out of Violet's pocket.

Across the field, a girl named Sara was getting ready to kick the ball.

"Go, Sara!" the crowd yelled.

Sara kicked the ball. Just like before, it flew all the way across the field. It soared right toward the net.

Violet and Sprite watched the ball closely. Violet thought she saw something.

A pair of wings.

"Did you see that?" Violet asked.

Sprite nodded.

The ball landed inside the net. The crowd cheered again. Violet saw something fly away from the ball.

"Hey, come back here!" Violet yelled.

It was a fairy, all right. But it was flying so fast Violet could barely see it.

Violet followed the fairy off the field and

into a group of trees. Sprite popped out of Violet's pocket.

"Stop, in the name of Queen Mab!" Sprite called out.

The fairy did a quick somersault in midair. She faced Sprite and Violet.

"A challenge," she said. "I like that!"

Violet looked at the pixie. She had white wings. Her dark hair was pulled into a pony-tail high on her head. Her blue eyes tilted ever so slightly. She wore a tank top with a number one on it, and tiny sneakers on her feet.

Sprite took a medal out of his bag and flew up to her.

"I am a Royal Pixie Tricker," he said bravely. "I order you to go back to the Otherworld."

The fairy smiled. "I'm Sport," she said.

"I'm a sprite. And if you're looking for a game, you've got one. Just don't expect to win!"

"This isn't a game," Sprite told her. "You can't go around enchanting sports equipment. It's just not right."

Sport flew in circles around Sprite. "Try to stop me!" she said.

Sprite tried to catch her. But he couldn't keep up.

Violet stepped between them.

"Excuse me," she said. "But I have a question."

Sport stopped flying.

"Shoot," she said.

"Most pixies like to mess things up," Violet said. "Like you messed up that equipment. But it looked like you were *helping* that soccer team."

"Of course I was," Sport said. "They're my team. And we're going to win every game!"

"But that's not fair," Violet said. "You can't use magic to win!"

Sport winked at her. "I'm a pixie. We like to mess things up, just like you said. Besides, the other girls don't know what I'm doing. I'm just helping them a little bit."

While Sport talked, Sprite fumbled in his bag. He wanted to find the *Book of Tricks.*

Sport didn't give Sprite or Violet a chance to do any tricking.

"Gotta fly!" she said. "My team needs me!"

Then she whizzed away.

Sprite started to fly after her, but Violet stopped him.

"She's too fast," Violet said. "We know where to find her when we're ready. Let's look in the book."

Sprite opened the book. Leon ran up to them.

"What are you doing all the way down here?" he asked.

"We found the fairy," Violet said. She told him all about Sport.

"Here's her page," Sprite said. He read the rhyme out loud:

"'Sport loves to cheat, she won't play fair.

To trick her, beat her fair and square.'"

"What does that mean?" Leon asked.

"I think we have to beat her in a game," Violet said. "But we can't cheat like she does."

"That's easy!" Leon said. "I can join the soccer league. I'll show her my magic moves." Leon dribbled an imaginary soccer ball.

"Leon, it's a *girl's* soccer league," Violet reminded him.

"Oh, yeah," Leon said.

Sprite flew around Violet's face excitedly.

"Then *you* can join the league!" Sprite said. "Your team can beat her team. Then she'll be tricked!"

"Me?" Violet wasn't so sure. She had fun playing soccer in gym class, but she didn't think she was so good at it. There were other things she was good at. Like playing the recorder. And tricking pixies.

"You've got to do it, Violet," Sprite said. "It's the only way!"

Violet sighed.

This day wasn't going at all the way she had planned. All she wanted was to do her homework — and eat some spaghetti.

Tricking pixies was so hard!

"Okay," Violet said. "I'll do it. I'll join the soccer league!"

Chapter Six
The Practice Game

"I think it's great you joined the soccer team," Violet's friend Brittany said. She twirled a strand of her long blond hair.

Violet's friend Tina kicked a soccer ball from one foot to the other.

"It's fun," Tina said. "Almost as fun as drawing and painting."

Violet couldn't believe she was part of the team. She felt weird in the uniform. She

wore a blue T-shirt, white shorts, long blue socks, shin guards, and soccer shoes.

"I don't know if I'm any good at this," Violet said.

Tina smiled. "Don't worry. My sister is a great coach."

Tina's older sister, Marisa, coached the team. Both Marisa and Tina had dark hair and big brown eyes. Marisa was tall and thin. She wore a whistle around her neck.

Violet relaxed a little. Marisa was nice. Maybe this wouldn't be so bad after all.

Marisa blew her whistle. The girls on the team gathered around her.

"Go, Blue Team!" Leon called from the stands. Sprite hid in Leon's jacket pocket.

"I'm glad to see some new faces on the team," Marisa said. She smiled at Violet. "As you know, to win in soccer you have to get the ball into the other team's goal. You can use your feet or your head."

Marisa bounced the ball off her head. Violet caught it.

"But you can't use your hands!" Marisa said. She smiled at Violet.

Violet blushed. This was the part Violet didn't like so much. She could do a lot of things with her hands. But she was always tripping over her feet.

Marisa put some orange cones in a line on the field.

"Moving the ball along the ground with your feet is called dribbling," she said. "Let's get in some dribbling practice."

Marisa put a soccer ball on the ground. She kicked it from foot to foot. She moved around each of the cones until she got to the end of the line.

"Let's line up and try it," Marisa said.

Violet made sure she got on the end of the line. One by one, the girls dribbled the ball between the cones. Some of the girls kicked the ball too hard or too far. But nobody laughed or made fun. They all did their best.

Soon it was Violet's turn. She slowly kicked the ball from one foot to the other.

"That's it, Violet," Marisa called out. "You can do it!"

Violet dribbled the ball faster. She darted around the cones. She was doing it!

Then, *wham*! Violet's two feet crossed. She fell facedown in the grass.

"Good work, Violet," Marisa said. "You're getting the hang of it."

Violet's face turned bright red. She got back in line.

"You're doing great," Tina told her.

But Violet wasn't so sure.

"Heads up, Violet!"

Violet spun around. Marisa threw a ball right to her. Violet quickly caught it.

"You have quick reflexes," Marisa said. "You just might be our goalie."

Goalie? Violet couldn't believe it. That was an important job. The goalie had to make sure the ball didn't get into the net. The goalie was the only player who could use her hands in the game.

The team practiced dribbling for a while. Then Marisa had them practice passing the ball to one another.

"You're right, Tina," Violet said. She kicked the ball to her friend. "This is pretty fun." The girls laughed and joked as they practiced. Then suddenly, everyone got quiet.

"What's the Red Team doing here?" Brittany asked.

Violet turned around. Twelve girls wearing red T-shirts stood at the other end of the field. The Red Team.

Sport's team!

Violet panicked. They couldn't play

Sport's team now. They didn't have enough practice!

A tall man with blond hair stood next to Mandy. Violet guessed it was Mandy's dad.

"We're here for the practice game," he said.

Marisa blew her whistle. "Coach Miles agreed to let our teams practice together," she said.

"But we're not ready," Violet said.

The other girls nodded in agreement. They didn't know about Sport. But they knew that the Red Team couldn't be beaten. They were good. Too good.

Marisa ruffled Violet's hair.

"It's just practice," she said. "We won't play a full game. Just one quarter."

Violet ran to Leon and Sprite.

"What should I do?" she asked.

"Beat them!" Leon said. "Beat them and get Sport out of here."

"I don't think it's going to be that easy," Violet said.

"Do your best," Sprite said. "I'll use magic to help."

Violet didn't like the sound of that. "Using magic would be cheating, wouldn't

it? I thought we couldn't cheat. The *Book of Tricks* said we have to beat her fair and square."

"If Sport uses magic, then it's only fair that I use magic, too," Sprite said.

"Yeah!" Leon agreed.

Violet shrugged.

Back on the field, Marisa blew her whistle. "Blue Team wins the coin toss," she said. "We get to kick off first."

"I have to go," Violet told Leon and Sprite.

Marisa picked seven girls to start the game. She made Violet goalie. She gave Violet a pair of goalie gloves to wear. Violet also put on a long-sleeved orange shirt, so the referee could tell her apart from the other players. Brittany and a girl named Jen were in front of the net. They were defenders.

They would help keep the ball away from the goal.

Tina and a girl named Kayla lined up by the center line. Marisa said they were forwards. Their job was to get the ball into the Red Team's goal.

Two more players, Lisa and April, lined up behind Tina and Kayla. Lisa and April were midfielders. They had to pass the ball to the forwards and help the defenders, too.

Violet looked up and down the field. No sign of Sport anywhere. But she had to be around. She just had to.

Tina moved to a circle in the middle of the field. Coach Miles put the ball on a line that divided the circle in half. Then he stepped away and blew his whistle.

Tina was fast. She dribbled the ball

around Mandy. Kayla ran down the field. Tina passed the ball to her.

Kayla dribbled to the goal. Tina ran ahead of Kayla. Then Kayla passed the ball back to her. Tina was right in front of the goal. She had a clear shot.

She kicked the ball with all her might.

Bam!

The soccer ball exploded into pieces!

Chapter Seven
Sport's Threat

Coach Miles blew his whistle.

The pieces of the ball floated onto the field like snowflakes.

"Whoa!" Marisa exclaimed. "That was some kick, Tina! What happened here?"

Coach Miles picked up the pieces. "Must have been a bad ball," he said, shaking his head. "What should we do now? This isn't in the rule book."

The two coaches looked stumped.

"Maybe a drop-in?" Marisa said.

"Sounds fair," Coach Miles said. He got a new ball and then called to one of the Red Team defenders. "Stacy, face off with Tina."

The red-haired girl and Tina faced each other.

"I'm going to drop the ball between you," Coach Miles said. "Whoever gets it first, after it touches the ground, has control of the ball."

Coach Miles dropped the ball. Tina was too shaken up to move fast enough. Stacy kicked the ball away from her.

Stacy kicked the ball to another Red Team member. Violet recognized the curly-haired girl. It was Sara, one of the girls who had kicked the ball so far the other day.

Sara dribbled to the middle of the field.

She could have passed the ball to a team-mate. Instead, she aimed for the goal. She kicked the ball as hard as she could.

The ball zoomed high in the air. Violet held her arms out, ready to catch the ball. It looked like it was coming right for her.

The ball started to drop down. Violet dove for it.

Then, suddenly, the ball made a sharp right turn. Violet grabbed an armful of air. The ball bounced into the net.

"Score, Red Team!" shouted Coach Miles.

Violet couldn't believe it. Neither could the Blue Team.

"That was weird!" Marisa said. "It's like the ball had wings or something."

Fairy wings, Violet thought. *Only Sport could do something like that.*

The rest of the practice game went like that. Every time Tina and Kayla got a shot at the Red Team goal, something weird happened to the ball. It shot straight up in the air. It circled around Kayla's head. Or it just wouldn't move.

"Something's wrong with this ball," Tina said, kicking it.

Coach Miles blew his whistle. He easily picked up the ball.

"Looks fine to me!" he said.

"Maybe there's a strong wind blowing on the field," Marisa said.

Every time the Red Team got the ball, they made goal shots from all over the field. Violet always thought she could stop the ball. But the ball always sneaked in.

Violet saw a flash of wings each time. She got angrier and angrier.

Violet waved her arms at Leon and Sprite.

Do something! she mouthed. They had to know the team needed help — fast.

Mandy kicked the ball at the goal. Violet dove to catch it.

Come on, Sprite, Violet thought. *Help me!*

From the corner of her eye, Violet saw a sprinkle of pixie dust outside Leon's pocket.

She threw her arms around the ball.

"Got it!" Violet cried.

Then she stopped.

One, two, three, four soccer balls appeared out of nowhere. They flew past Violet and landed inside the net.

"Score!" Coach Miles yelled. "Game over! Red Team wins, nine to zero."

The girls on the Red Team cheered.

Violet and the Blue Team ran up to Marisa.

"Where did all those balls come from?" Brittany asked.

Marisa looked upset. "I'm not sure. Maybe they rolled out of the equipment bag."

"I still think there is something wrong with that ball," Tina said.

"I'll check all the equipment before our next practice," Marisa said. "Something's not right, that's for sure."

Violet wished she could tell everyone about Sport. But she couldn't. She had to keep all the pixies a secret.

Violet felt something soft brush against her face. She heard a little laugh.

"Sport!" she said under her breath. She ran after the fairy. Leon and Sprite saw her and followed.

Sport was swinging from a tree branch, wearing a big smile.

"We won!" she cried. "My team is number one!"

"You didn't play fair!" Violet said. "You cheated the whole time."

"That's how you see it," Sport said. "I'm just using my skills to win. Besides, Sprite tried to use some magic."

Sprite hung his head. "I did try. But it didn't work. All those soccer balls came out of nowhere! I guess I'm not supposed to use magic."

Sport laughed. "This is great! I can use magic to beat you. But you can't use it to beat me. You'll never win!"

"We will win!" Sprite said, flying up to Sport. "If anyone can do it, Violet can."

"We'll see about that," Sport said. "Until then, I'll keep messing up sports equipment everywhere!"

Chapter Eight
The Sock Thief Returns

"That was a good practice today," Sprite told Violet a few nights later.

Violet nodded. She and the team had been working hard. They practiced three days a week. But tomorrow was their first real game.

They would face the Red Team again.

"We're good," Violet said. She folded the uniform that her mom had just washed. "But we're not good enough to beat Sport's magic. No one is."

She sank down on her bed.

Sprite flew in front of her face. "You can do it, Violet. I know you can."

Just then, the door flew open. Leon burst into the room. A pair of antennae bobbed on his head.

"What do you think?" Leon asked.

"Think about what?" Violet replied.

Leon pointed to the antennae. "It's my costume," he said. "I'm the team mascot. The Blue Beetle."

Sprite flew around Leon. "You don't look like any of the beetles I know," Sprite said.

"I figured if I have to go to all your games, I should have something to do," Leon explained.

Normally, Violet would have thought Leon's idea was pretty funny. But she didn't think anything was funny right now.

Leon noticed. "What's wrong?" he asked.

"We'll never win that game tomorrow," Violet said. "No matter how hard we try."

"Why don't you ask that fairy queen lady what to do?" Leon asked. "She's always telling you how to fix stuff."

Sprite smiled. "Leon, that's a great idea!"

Sprite reached into his bag. He took out a purple stone.

"Queen Mab, we need you," Sprite said.

The stone glowed with soft purple light. Then the beautiful fairy appeared. Queen Mab had red hair and purple eyes — the same color as Violet's eyes.

"I'm here, Sprite," the queen said. "What do you need?"

Violet picked up the stone. "It's Sport, Your Majesty," she said. "My soccer team

has to beat her team. But Sport uses magic. There's no way we can win!"

Queen Mab smiled. "You have an advantage, Violet," she said. "You know what Sport is going to do."

"How does that help?" Violet asked.

The queen looked at Sprite. "Don't forget. You can always turn Sport's magic against her."

"But Queen Mab —" Violet began.

The purple light faded. The queen's face vanished.

"What did the queen mean by all that stuff?" Leon asked.

Violet yawned. "I'm not sure," she said. "I'll think about it in the morning. I'm sleepy now. And there's a big game tomorrow."

Leon left. Sprite curled up among the soft socks in Violet's sock drawer. Violet climbed into bed and turned out the light.

The next morning, Violet picked at her breakfast. All she could think about was the game.

Soon it was time to get into uniform. Violet put on her orange shirt and her white shorts. Then she looked in her drawer to find her special blue socks.

She found Sprite, still asleep. And she found one blue sock.

One sock was missing!

"Wake up, Sprite," Violet said. "Have you seen my other blue sock? I need it. It's part of my soccer uniform."

Sprite rubbed his eyes. "Blue sock? No. I don't think so. What would I want with a sock, anyway? I'm not —"

"Ragamuffin!" Violet cried. She had almost forgotten about the sock-stealing pixie.

There was a puff of pixie dust, and Ragamuffin appeared. She held the missing sock in her hand.

"Hi, guys!" she said cheerfully. "Isn't this sock super?"

"That's my sock," Violet said. "I need it for my soccer uniform. May I please have it back?"

Ragamuffin pouted. "But it's so pretty. It's blue. Like the sky. Or a blue beetle. It's just super."

Then Violet remembered. "Ragamuffin, do you still have those cool clothes I gave you the other day?"

Ragamuffin nodded. She dug through a patchwork pouch she kept slung around her shoulder.

"They're in here somewhere," Ragamuffin said. Then she pulled out the purple outfit. "Here!"

"That outfit is much nicer than my old sock," Violet said. "Why don't you try it on?"

Ragamuffin shrugged. "Why not?" She put down Violet's sock. Then the pixie reached into one of her pockets. She took out some pixie dust.

Ragamuffin sprinkled the pixie dust on herself. *Poof!* Her crazy-colored outfit was gone. Now she wore the white-and-purple outfit Violet had given her. The perfectly matched outfit.

A swirling tunnel of wind appeared behind Ragamuffin. The wind picked up the pixie. It pulled her inside the tunnel.

Violet and Sprite smiled at each other.

Ragamuffin was going back to the Otherworld. They had tricked her!

"This is not very super!" Ragamuffin cried. Then the wind tunnel vanished.

Sprite opened up the *Book of Tricks*. Ragamuffin's picture was in the book, next to her rhyme. That meant the trick had worked.

"We did it!" Sprite said happily.

"We sure did," Violet said. "And now we've got to go trick Sport. We've got a game to win!"

Chapter Nine
A Wizard in the Crowd

"I know we lost to the Red Team during a practice game," Marisa told the team. "But don't let that get you down. You've all been practicing very hard. You can win this!"

Violet, Brittany, Tina, and the other girls on the Blue Team looked at one another. They knew they had worked hard. They knew they were good.

But nobody had beaten the Red Team yet. How could they?

Marisa smiled at them. "Get out there and warm up," she told the girls. "It's almost game time."

Violet started to run onto the field. Then she felt a strange tingling on the back of her neck.

Violet turned around. A tall man with white hair was sitting in the stands. The people around him wore T-shirts that said WIZ FINNSTER FOR MAYOR.

The man looked right at Violet.

Violet felt cold all over. She couldn't move.

It was Finn the Wizard! The wizard who led the fairy escape. Finn was running for mayor. He was trying to take over the whole town.

But nobody knew he was a wicked

wizard. Nobody except for Violet, Leon, and Sprite.

"Hey, Violet, what's the matter?" Leon asked, jumping in front of her. His antennae bounced on his head.

Sprite poked his head out of Leon's pocket.

"It's Finn — Finn the Wizard," Violet whispered. "He's in the stands. He knows who I am. I can tell."

Leon started to turn around.

"No!" Violet cried. "I don't want him to know we're talking about him. What if he gets mad? What if he casts a spell on us or something?"

"I'm sure Finn wouldn't do anything out in the open like this," Sprite said. "There are too many people around."

Violet wasn't so sure. She held her stomach. "I don't feel so good. I don't think I can play."

"You have to," Sprite said. "You have to win the game and trick Sport."

"I don't think I can do it," Violet said.

Then loud voices cheered from the stands.

"Yay, Violet!"

Violet looked up. It was her mom and dad. And Leon's mom, Aunt Anne. They had all come to see her play.

"They believe in you," Sprite said. "I do, too."

Sprite flew out of Leon's pocket and hid behind one of Violet's brown braids.

"I'll stay with you," he said. "No one will see me from so far away. I'll make sure nothing bad happens."

Violet took a deep breath. "Okay," she said. "See you later, Blue Beetle."

"Right!" Leon said.

Violet ran out onto the field. The girls on her team were passing the ball back and forth to one another. Violet joined in. But her mind was on Sport the whole time.

The queen said I could beat Sport be-

cause I know what she will do, Violet thought. *What did she mean by that?*

And then, like lightning, it hit her.

"I know what to do," she whispered to Sprite. "I know how to beat Sport at her own game!"

Chapter Ten
The Big Game

The Red Team won the coin toss. Mandy stood in the center circle. A referee placed the ball in front of her. Then he ran to the sidelines.

Tweet! the whistle blew. Sara ran to the Blue Team's side of the field. Mandy kicked the ball to her.

Sara dribbled the ball down the field. Brittany and Jen ran in front of her, trying to keep her away from the goal. Sara passed the ball to Mandy on the other side of the field.

Mandy had a clear shot to the goal. Violet bent down, hands on her knees, waiting for action.

She really did know how to outsmart Sport. It was easy. Violet knew that if Mandy kicked the ball to Violet's right, Sport would make the ball change direction at the last second.

Whack! Mandy gave the ball a hard kick toward the goal.

Violet pretended to dive after the ball. But at the last second, she dove in the other direction.

The ball changed direction at the same time. Violet was ready. She leaned into the ball. It bounced off her chest and back onto the field.

"Go, Violet, go!" Leon yelled from the sidelines.

Jen ran to the ball and started dribbling it up the field. The Blue Team had the ball!

"Good job, Violet!" Sprite said.

"The Red Team won't be able to score a goal off of me," Violet said. "Not if I can help it."

Jen passed the ball to April. April passed the ball to Lisa.

Tina dodged around the Red Team's defenders. She broke free. Lisa passed the ball to Tina.

Tina dribbled the ball closer to the goal. She had a clear shot.

Whack! Tina gave the ball a hard kick.

The ball rolled across the grass. The Red Team goalie ran after it. But she was too far away.

"We're going to score!" Violet yelled.

But at the last second, the ball rose in the air, like someone was picking it up. It flew away from the goal and landed outside the white line.

Tweet! The referee's whistle blew.

"Out of bounds!" yelled the referee. "Red Team gets a throw-in."

The Red Team goalie stood outside the line, where the ball landed. She picked up the ball and threw it with both hands to one of her teammates.

The Red Team dribbled and passed the ball down the field. Violet waited, ready to stop Sport again.

This time, Sara took a shot at the goal. Violet locked her eyes on the ball. As soon as the ball changed direction, she reached out and grabbed it.

"Yay, Violet!" Leon yelled again.

"Drat!" Violet heard a little voice say. Then she saw two flapping wings fly away from the ball.

Violet smiled at Leon and kicked the ball to Brittany. Keeping up with Sport wasn't easy. She hoped she could last the game.

The girls on the Blue Team took the ball to the Red Team's side. This time, Kayla had a clear shot at the goal. She aimed. She kicked. . . .

Whoosh! The ball flew up and went backward over Kayla's head!

Violet knew Kayla was a good player. That was Sport at work again.

The Red Team had the ball again. But the referee's whistle blew.

"First quarter is over!" he cried. "Two-minute break."

Only three more quarters to go, Violet realized.

"You're doing great, Violet," Sprite told her.

Violet shook her head. "It doesn't matter. I can keep the Red Team from scoring. But if the Blue Team doesn't score, then the game will end in a tie. We won't win. We'll never get rid of Sport!"

Chapter Eleven
Trops, Trops, Trops!

"There has to be some way," Sprite said. "Don't worry. I'll think of something."

"Don't waste your time!"

Sprite and Violet jumped. It was Sport.

"I know what you're up to," Sport said. "You won't win this game. You won't send me back!"

Then, in a flash, she flew away.

The referee's whistle blew. The two teams took their places.

The second and third quarters went a lot like the first. Violet made sure the Red Team couldn't score a goal, no matter how hard they tried. And Sport made sure the Blue Team could not score, no matter how hard *they* tried.

Thanks to Sport's magic, Kayla's shoes came untied as she dribbled the ball. A cloud of dust blew into Tina's eyes as she was about to kick a goal. She missed the ball completely.

Jen tripped and bumped into a Red Team player. The referee called a foul and gave the Red Team a free kick.

By the time the third quarter ended, the Blue Team was exhausted. The score was still zero to zero.

"I know we've been having some bad luck out there," Marisa said. "But you guys are doing great."

It's more than bad luck! Violet wanted to shout. *There's a bad fairy who's cheating! It's not fair!*

But she couldn't tell anyone. All she could do was go out there and do her best.

Marisa sent the team back onto the field. Sprite waited on the net for Violet. From a distance, he looked like a shiny green bug.

"Have you thought of anything yet?" Violet asked.

"I'm not sure," Sprite said. "The queen said we should use Sport's magic against her. But I'm not sure how. Sometimes Sport makes the ball move left. Sometimes it goes right. Sometimes it goes backwards —"

"Backwards!" Violet shouted. "That's it! We can say Sport's name backwards three times. That stops pixie magic, doesn't it?"

"For a little bit," Sprite said. "It could work. We'd have to keep saying it, though."

"Go tell Leon," Violet said.

Sprite darted across the field and landed on Leon's shoulder. Sprite whispered something in Leon's ear. Then Leon jumped up and chanted, "Trops! Trops! Trops!"

Brittany looked at Violet. "Why is Leon saying that?" she asked.

"It's a good luck cheer," Violet said. "It might help get rid of our bad luck. You have to say it three times in a row."

Brittany shrugged. "Sounds good to me," she said. "Trops, trops, trops!"

Soon word got down the field to the other Blue Team members.

"Trops, trops, trops!" they chanted.

Violet watched as the Blue Team passed

the ball back and forth. Now Tina had a shot at the Red Team goal.

Violet could see Sport flapping around Tina's head. The fairy looked like a white moth. Her wings were beating wildly.

Tina aimed for the goal. "Trops, trops, trops!" she cried.

Tina kicked the ball. It zoomed across the grass.

Tweet! "Goal, Blue Team!" the referee shouted.

"Yay, Tina!" Violet yelled. It worked! Sport had tried to use magic to stop Tina. But she couldn't.

"Trops, trops, trops!" Violet chanted.

Sport flew up to Violet.

"This isn't fair!" Sport hissed in her ear. "I can't use my magic!"

"Don't you see?" Violet asked. "Now it finally *is* fair. Fair and square."

Both teams played their best. There wasn't much time left in the quarter. Soon, the referee blew his whistle for the last time.

"Game!" he called out. "Blue Team wins, one to zero!"

Violet felt a wind blow on the back of her

neck. She looked behind her. Sport was disappearing inside a tunnel of wind.

"No faaaaaaaair!" Sport cried. Then *poof*! The tunnel vanished.

Violet ran to the center of the field. The girls on the Blue Team hugged one another.

"Let's shake hands with the Red Team," Marisa said. "They played a great game."

When they were done, Violet looked into the stands. Her mom, dad, and Aunt Anne clapped and waved. Finn the Wizard stormed out of the stands. He looked angry.

Violet didn't want to think of that right now. She ran up to Leon. Sprite was tucked back inside Leon's pocket.

"Thanks, Leon," Violet said. "You're a great mascot."

"I saved the day again, of course," Leon

said. "I guess you can quit the team now, right?"

"Quit?" Violet asked. "What do you mean?"

"I thought you only joined to trick Sport," Leon said. "We tricked her. So you don't have to play anymore."

"I think I'll keep playing," Violet said. "It's fun!"

Sprite peeked out of the pocket. "More fun than tricking fairies with me?"

"Almost," Violet said. "But I'll always have time for you."

Sprite blushed.

"Thanks," he said. "Should we go look for some fairies now?"

"I think I've had enough excitement for one day," Violet said. "Maybe tomorrow."

"Tomorrow, then," Sprite said. "We still have five more pixies to trick!"

Pixie Tricks Stickers

Place the stickers in the *Book of Tricks*. You can find your very own copy of the *Book of Tricks* in the first two books of the Pixie Tricks series, *Sprite's Secret* and *The Greedy Gremlin*. When Sprite and Violet catch a pixie, stick its sticker in the book. Follow the directions in the *Book of Tricks* to complete each pixie's page. (Pixie Secret: Some of these pixies haven't been caught yet. Save their stickers to use later.)

·.·PiXiE·TRiCKS·.·

Seeing Is Believing!

Available wherever you buy books, or use this order form.

❑ BFB 0-439-17218-7   **#1: Sprite's Secret** $3.99 U.S.
❑ BFB 0-439-17219-5   **#2: The Greedy Gremlin** $3.99 U.S.
❑ BFB 0-439-17978-5   **#3: The Pet Store Sprite** $3.99 U.S.
❑ BFB 0-439-07980-7   **#4: The Halloween Goblin** $3.99 U.S.
❑ BFB 0-439-17981-5   **#5: The Angry Elf** $3.99 U.S.

Scholastic Inc., P.O. Box 7502, Jefferson City, MO 65102

Please send me the books I have checked above. I am enclosing $_____ (please add $2.00 to cover shipping and handling). Send check or money order—no cash or C.O.D.s please.

Name_____Birth date_____

Address_____

City_____State/Zip_____

Please allow four to six weeks for delivery. Offer good in U.S.A. only. Sorry, mail orders are not available to residents of Canada. Prices subject to change.

PIX1100

visit us at www.scholastic.com